Saving Kennedy

- J.L. Pattison -

Two short stories about time travel, the JFK assassination, and the consequences of the choices we make.

Alibi Interrupted
&
The Visitor

<u>Praise for *Saving Kennedy*</u>

"Possibly the best short story I have read!"
- *Anne*

"If you are a fan of the Twilight Zone this book is for you."
- *John Cavallone*

"My heart is still racing after just reading this story."
- *Patti Jane*

"I was blown away. It was amazing and scary at
the same time. *The Visitor* left me breathless."
- *Chris & Michelle Bledsoe*

"If the Twilight Zone still existed, [*The Visitor*] would be an
episode, it is that good. . . . *The Visitor* is [a] great read and
renews my love for the short story."
- *Papa Philly*

"Pattison's books are the kind that really remind you why you
love reading. . . . That's how it felt with *Alibi Interrupted*–
like I was reading something indisputably great."
- *Olivia Emily*

"Loved it. I seriously couldn't get enough of it. . . . There is
literally nothing else I can say other than perfection."
- *Cayli*

[*Alibi Interrupted*] is basically The Twilight Zone
meets [Stephen King's] 11/22/63 . . . . [It] gave me
chills. So many twists and turns and things you had to
think about. . . . It was perfect. Period."
- *Kester Nucum*

"I've read some good, some bad, and a lot of mediocre works through the years. J.L. Pattison has a good command of language, plot, characters, and dialogue. His writing is on par with some long-established authors . . . . He writes with a flair reminiscent of Rod Serling."
- Larry C.

"A time travel story that was ultimately distressingly realistic."
- *J.L. Gribble*

"The plot is compelling - I imagine Rod Sterling could adapt it quite nicely for an episode of the Twilight Zone."
- *Jay Eldred*

"J.L.'s ability to capture an entire sci-fi / mystery / time travel thriller . . . is nothing short of amazing."
- *Mark Escalera Sr.*

"This would be a great episode for a Twilight Zone . . ."
- *Meg Verity*

"Prepare your mind to be challenged ethically with a storyline that will leave you wanting more."
- *Stewart Brogden*

"Very well written in a manner that kept me riveted to the end."
- *Paul Bayne*

"That ending [of *The Visitor*] was probably one of the best (and creepiest) I have ever read. I love . . . twist endings . . . and it felt so eerie and Twilight Zone-ish."
- *Kester Nucum*

Copyright © 2016 J.L. Pattison

Saving Kennedy
Cover concept: J.L. Pattison
Cover artist: Ozzy Art
Cover designer: Suzette Vaughn

Alibi Interrupted
Editor: Shani Dues
Cover designer: Marty Dues

The Visitor
Editor: Sony Elise
Cover designer: Angie Alaya

The two stories contained in *Saving Kennedy* (*Alibi Interrupted* and *The Visitor*) are works of fiction. All elements of these works of fiction are drawn from the author's imagination. Where real people, places, events, establishments, businesses, or organizations appear, they are used fictitiously.

To my wife.

I'm still in awe of your dedication, love, and patience.

To my children.

I am honored to be your daddy, and it is my sincere prayer that my decisions in life—both small and large—will always be wise, make you proud, and be worthy of your emulation.

Alibi Interrupted

J.L. Pattison

Alibi Interrupted

J.L. Pattison

Part 1 - The Alibi

~~~
ONE
~~~

Because he was going to be born next year, Stewart Hudson knew he had to die by the end of this summer. This wasn't due to any belief in the fabled tales of reincarnation; it was a consequence of time travel gone wrong.

Today, Stewart's mind was occupied with the secret he was about to reveal, a secret he always thought he'd take to the grave.

When Kohen arrived at Stewart's house, he let himself in, finding Stewart in the study surrounded from floor to ceiling by neatly shelved books. Kohen took a seat next to the old man whose frail hands lay folded over an old shoebox resting on his lap.

Skipping the small talk, Kohen declined Stewart's offer of tea or coffee in lieu of getting down to business. He was not there for one of his regular visits, he was there to find out the truth. He deserved to know the truth—the whole family did.

Kohen opened this can of worms a week earlier when he called to ask questions about Stewart's past, or the lack thereof. He'd been researching their family tree

7

for a genealogy assignment for his degree but couldn't find any record of Stewart prior to the mid-1960s.

Because Stewart would never give a straight answer, the family stopped asking long ago about the patriarch's past. Kohen was the exception. He was the most stubborn of all those in Stewart's lineage and he would no longer accept the silence. When Kohen Hudson set out on a task he wouldn't come up for air until it was accomplished, and now his own grandfather was in his crosshairs.

Before he began, Stewart made Kohen agree not to tell anyone in the family. It would be easier for them to continue assuming Stewart was concealing a criminal past than it would be to expect them to believe his story. An early life of crime was certainly a less complex and a more believable explanation than the truth.

So, here they were. Grandfather and grandson, sitting in the midst of thousands of books where only a small table, a long generation, and a carefully guarded secret separated them.

"It all started," Stewart said, drawing a deep breath, "the day I traveled back in time to change history."

~~~
# TWO
~~~

I trembled as I took in my surroundings. I couldn't believe I was here, I mean *really* here. I visited this location many times in the future, but now I was here the precise moment history was about to be made and the precise moment this place was about to become known to the world.

And that's exactly why I was here: to make sure history *wasn't* made. To ensure that Dealey Plaza remained known only to locals and that November 22, 1963, would be just another ordinary day in Dallas.

I thought I was prepared to do this. I expected to execute my mission in a systematic and methodical fashion, but as I emerged from under the triple overpass I saw the Texas School Book Depository and froze. Truth is, I was woefully unprepared for this.

Seconds after my arrival I realized that I failed to take into account how the impact of being here would affect me. I never considered myself an emotional man, but now I found myself using the back of my hand to wipe away the welling of tears in my eyes.

As far back as I can remember, I've always been captivated with the history of the assassination of President John F. Kennedy. Maybe it was because I was born and raised in Dallas. Maybe it was because I was born at Parkland Hospital where both Kennedy and Oswald were taken after being shot. Or perhaps it was because I shared a birthday on May 29th with JFK— albeit, over a century apart.

When other kids my age were consumed with entertainment, I was reading everything I could about the assassination. And now at just 20 years old, while my peers were tethered to their phones sharing pictures of themselves, their pets, and their lunch with the world, I was about to *change* the world.

And thanks to the technology of time travel, here I was in Dealey Plaza just minutes from one of the biggest events in American history. It was an odd feeling knowing that at this moment in time Kennedy was still alive, and if I was successful, he would remain that way.

I peered at the clock that comprised a large portion of the car rental billboard sitting atop the Book Depository. The time read 12:19. I had less than eleven minutes to do what needed to be done. I checked my wristwatch and discovered its hands were frozen in place. It did not survive the time trip.

Pushing aside the debilitating weight of the historical significance of where I was and what I was about to do, I placed one foot in front of the other in the direction of the Book Depository.

My hope was to enter the infamous brick building without being noticed. If I kept my head down and acted natural I'd be able to get to the sixth floor without any problems. But if I did arouse suspicion I was prepared with a backstory: my boss sent me to fix a leaky pipe on the sixth floor. I even carried a fake work order in my pocket.

I didn't expect to be answering any questions though. After all, no one knew what was about to happen so no one would be suspicious of me. Unless, of course, I failed and the president was slain. Then my presence in the building would be highly suspicious. It wouldn't take long for authorities to figure out that I was not a plumber, there was no water leak on the sixth floor, and I didn't work for a company named *Lone Star Plumbing*.

At the very least I'd be taken downtown for questioning, but what would I tell them? I was there to stop the assassination of the president? That would show I had prior knowledge and would only make matters worse.

Of course, if I told them my prior knowledge of the assassination was due to the fact that I was from the future, they'd put me in a straitjacket. So, in the event I was detained, my only hope of escape would be to activate my recall module before anyone could stop me.

Concealed under my clothing, the recall module hung around my neck on a chain. Depressing the button on top of the metallic cylinder would begin my return to the future.

If the cops prevented me from activating it, I'd be stuck in 1963. And if a cop took possession of it and pressed the button, he'd find himself transported into the future. What a shock that would be for him, not to mention my friends awaiting my return at the lab.

As I made my way up the sidewalk, approaching the Stemmons Freeway sign, I glanced over my left shoulder toward the pedestal where Abraham Zapruder was preparing to capture the presidential motorcade on film. That's when I bumped into the only man in Dealey Plaza carrying an umbrella, knocking it out of his hands. I apologized as I kept walking but he only glared at me, clearly unhappy about my inattention.

How careless could I be? For not wanting to be noticed I was already doing a poor job, and I wasn't even in the building yet.

I reassured myself that my plan was foolproof; nothing could go wrong. I'd enter the building undetected and by the time anyone realized what happened, I'd be gone.

I had been meticulous about my appearance. My hair was sheered in a crew cut style common for 1963 and I was dressed in forest green coveralls. *Stewart* was embroidered on a patch over my left breast and *Lone Star Plumbing* was stitched across my back.

You'd be surprised how hard it was to find a late 1950s, early 1960s toolbox in the mid-21st Century. Even the watch I wore was vintage 1958. I spared no expense in appearing like I belonged in 1963. The success of my mission depended on it.

Cutting my arrival time close was a tactical move. It was important to avoid getting inside the Book Depository too soon because having too much time in the building beforehand would increase my chances of being discovered. I just needed enough time to get inside, ascend to the sixth floor, and incapacitate the would-be assassin. If my mission was a success, someone would find Lee Harvey Oswald's body behind boxes of books next to his rifle on the sixth floor.

I weaved my way through the excited throng of onlookers that were assembled on the corner of Elm Street and Houston Street, and found myself at the entrance of the Book Depository.

Swallowing deeply, I ascended the steps to enter the building as butterflies danced with reckless abandon in my stomach. Once inside, I noticed my hands visibly shaking. I avoided eye contact and sought out the stairwell that was to my immediate right.

Those stairs were how I intended to reach the sixth floor where I would approach Oswald from behind and, with the heavy wrench concealed in my toolbox, do what was necessary.

The best case scenario is I'd knock him unconscious; worst case scenario, he would never come to. Either way, I was prepared to do what needed to be done. After all, I was saving the president's life. If there was ever a quintessential example of the end justifying the means, this was it.

As I raised my foot to place it on the first step, a man brushed past me as he headed up the stairs. "Excuse me," he said through a mouthful of food.

When our eyes met I drew an audible gasp of air. It was Lee Harvey Oswald.

~~~
## THREE
~~~

Everything inside me seized, including my breathing. My mouth went dry and my throat tightened as I stood frozen at the bottom of the steps watching Oswald ascend the stairs.

That face. My whole life it had stared back at me from photographs in history books and old black and white news reels. Now here I was, watching this man climb the stairs who—without my intervention—was about to kill the president.

Only seconds passed but it felt like an eternity before I regained my mental composure. My plans had changed. Oswald would never make it to the sniper's nest. His body would be found in the stairwell.

I removed the wrench from my toolbox and sprinted up the stairs to catch up to Oswald when he unexpectedly exited the stairwell on the second floor. *What could he possibly be doing?*

Without hesitation I burst onto the second floor in time to see Oswald disappear through two doors. *Perhaps he was retrieving his rifle from a hiding place.*

The thought of retreating to the stairs to await his return crossed my mind but was immediately pushed aside by the concern that he might take an alternate route to the sixth floor and I'd miss him while I was waiting.

I determined I would make my move the first opportunity I got no matter where Oswald was. Currently he was in my sights and I was not going to lose him. With my toolbox in one hand and the wrench in the other, I pursued him.

I burst into a lunchroom where I found Oswald gazing at a soda machine. I hadn't expected to gain on him so quickly, and my frantic entrance—coupled with my abrupt attempt to now appear casual—did not escape his notice.

Along the length of the lunchroom to my right was a wall of tables and chairs that also spanned the back wall. A vending machine stood to my immediate left whose front faced into the center of the room, toward Oswald. On the other side of the vending machine were wooden cabinets and above them was a clock that read 12:29. *It must have been fast because the president was to be shot at 12:30.*

Further ahead—past the cabinets—was a refrigerator, and next to the refrigerator was the soda machine where Oswald was making his selection. *But why was he concerning himself with buying a soda just minutes before he was going to assassinate the president?*

Improvising, I walked to my left and placed my toolbox and the wrench on the cabinet counter. There was enough space between the cabinets and the vending machine for me to stand so I took possession of that space like I just conquered a mountain.

Without hesitation I reached behind the vending machine to appear as if I was tinkering with something. This would be a sufficient cover as long as Oswald didn't see the word *plumbing* emblazoned across my back.

From the safety of the narrow space I occupied, only a few steps separated me from the would-be assassin. I could be on him before he realized what was happening but he would surely not go down without a fight. If someone walked into the room at that moment and intervened, I may not only fail to incapacitate Oswald, but I might be prevented from activating the recall module.

I reconsidered my options. I could wait till he returned to the stairwell and strike him down there, but if I exited right after he leaves the lunchroom he'd know I was following him and my element of surprise would be gone.

I even entertained the idea of allowing him a head start to go upstairs where I'd sneak up on him at the window on the sixth floor like my original plan. But what if I was delayed for some reason? What if a door I needed to get through was locked?

No. I couldn't take that chance. Reminding myself that it would be best to not lose sight of him, I determined that what I came here to do would have to be done in this very room.

When he makes his way to the door, I'd spring around the vending machine and strike him from behind. He wouldn't put up a fight because he wouldn't see it coming. Then I'd pull out the module and activate it. I would disappear into the future leaving Oswald to be found—dead or alive—on the floor. And if the cops found my fingerprints on scene they'd be unable to make a match because I hadn't even been born yet.

So, it came down to this moment. I was alone with Lee Harvey Oswald, the world's most famous assassin, and this very room is where I would change history.

Forgetting it didn't work, I glanced at my wristwatch again before checking the clock above the cabinets. The clock read 12:31. *Yep, it was fast.*

I continued to fiddle with the air behind the vending machine as Oswald retrieved a bottle from the soda machine. He would have to leave immediately to make it to the sniper's nest on time, but he appeared to be in no hurry.

As he removed the cap from the soda and placed the bottle to his lips, I picked up my wrench. *Any second now.* Sweat beaded on my forehead. I was the only person standing between Oswald and history.

But why wasn't he leaving? He needed to be in position on the sixth floor at this moment but he didn't seem to be in any rush. He just stood there sipping his soda as if he was waiting for someone or something.

Our eyes met again as I continued to tinker with the back of the vending machine. *Why was he cutting his time so short?*

My thoughts were interrupted by the door to the lunchroom swinging open. "Do you know this guy?" a panicked voice thundered. Oswald turned to face the doorway.

My presence was concealed by the vending machine from whoever was at the door. Utilizing the gap between the back of the vending machine and the wall I could see a uniformed arm protruding into the room holding a gun. It was a cop.

"Yes, he works here," another voice sounded from outside the room before the door closed and the two men were gone.

I knew my JFK assassination history well enough to know the man with the gun was Dallas Police Officer,

Marrion Baker and the voice of the man vouching for Oswald belonged to Book Depository superintendent, Roy Truly. I also knew that these two men didn't confront Oswald in the lunchroom until *after* the president was shot. But that was impossible. Oswald had been here with me.

The epiphany struck like lightening and my mouth responded without thinking. "So you *didn't* shoot the president?" I said out loud.

Oswald cast a brief glare at me before leaving the lunchroom.

I could hear my heart pounding in my ears as I threw my wrench into the toolbox, slammed the lid, and bolted from the room. I wanted to get downstairs as fast as possible but I was cognizant that rushing anywhere right now would draw unneeded attention. I forced myself to slow down and appear natural, whatever *natural* was in this situation.

When I arrived on the first floor I headed toward the set of stairs that led to the sidewalk outside.

I saw Oswald in front of me stop briefly to exchange a few words with a man in a suit who just entered the building. Oswald continued outside as the man, wearing a White House press badge, rushed past me.

Once outside my attention was immediately drawn to the chaos surrounding me. Droves of people were scattered throughout Dealey Plaza, a large portion of which were gathered on and around the grassy knoll.

I stood motionless watching history unfold before my eyes. Then it dawned on me: *I must warn Oswald that he was about to be set up.*

I turned back toward the Book Depository to find him but he was gone. I scanned the faces in the crowd but could not find him.

In a matter of seconds I went from Oswald's killer to Oswald's alibi. My mission was no longer to save the president, now I had to save Oswald.

FOUR

"But history tells me Oswald was arrested, then killed," Kohen interrupted.

"That's correct," Stewart said. "You know your history."

"I've always enjoyed history, it's one of my favorite subjects."

"You got your love of history from me."

"After it skipped a generation."

Stewart laughed.

"This is hard for me to believe," Kohen said. "And I don't understand what this has to do with your early life being shrouded in secrecy."

"Bear with me, it will all make sense."

"Ok, so what happened with Oswald?"

"I knew he was going to be arrested at the Texas Theater, so I hailed a taxi to take me there."

"You had money?"

"No. Since I hadn't found any money that was printed prior to 1963, I didn't bring any with me on the trip. And I didn't try very hard either because I didn't plan to be in 1963 for more than twenty minutes."

"It's better to have and not need than to need and not have is what my dad always said."

"Who do you think taught him that?"

Kohen smiled.

"So, anyway, I offered the driver my wristwatch in exchange for transportation and, after examining it for an agonizingly long time, he agreed to the deal, but with a caveat. He liked the watch, but because it didn't work he told me the deal was only worth taking me half way. Since I was running out of time I also offered him my toolbox and the wrench in exchange for taking me farther. He agreed to the deal and was gracious enough to take me a few blocks more."

"Closer to the theater?"

"Yes, but I was on foot the rest of the way. I thought I was making good time but I got there too late. When I arrived the outside of the Texas Theater was crowded with a large number of police officers and bystanders."

"Did you see Oswald?"

"Yes. As I made my way through the crowd I caught a glimpse of him being shoved into a police car and driven off."

"That was your best opportunity," Kohen said. "It would be much harder to warn him once he was in custody."

"That's true. The only other time I'd have any possibility of reaching him would be two days later in the police basement parking garage where he would be shot by Jack Ruby."

"Did you try to reach him there?"

"Kind of. It was too late to warn Oswald that he was going to be a patsy, he already had that figured out. Now I was just trying to save his life, or at least prolong the inevitable, by stopping Ruby."

Stewart fiddled with the frayed edges of the shoebox on his lap while Kohen leaned forward in his seat.

"I spent the next two nights sleeping where I could and panhandling for enough money to eat," Stewart said. "On the day Oswald was going to be shot I arrived at

21

one of the two street level entrances to the basement parking garage of the police department. I chose the one that history books suggested Ruby walked down to reach Oswald. It was shortly before noon and I watched for Ruby, hoping that I could stall him long enough to prevent what was going to happen."

"It's safe to assume you were unsuccessful."

"After some time had passed I approached one of the cops standing at the entrance to the basement. I asked him what time it was and he told me 12:15. I had five minutes to stop Oswald's murder. I looked around the street and sidewalk one last time. I saw no sign of Ruby anywhere, so if he was already in the basement he had to have gained access a different way. I felt I had no choice but to tell the cop that Oswald was about to be shot."

"Did he believe you?"

"Of course not. And being a disheveled mess from living on the street for the previous two days didn't help my credibility either. I pleaded with him to let someone know they had to stop, or at least delay, the transport of Oswald. But the more I made my case the more irritated the cop became with me. With no options left, I attempted to run past him and down the basement ramp."

"I don't see this ending very well."

"It wasn't the best of ideas but I was desperate. I made it about twenty feet before he took hold of me by the rear of my collar and jerked me backward into his arms. As he subdued me in a bear hug from behind, a horn blast emitted from the bowels of the basement parking garage followed by a single gunshot and the sound of commotion. Shoving me to the ground and instructing me to remain there till he got back, the cop darted down the ramp into the basement."

"Please tell me you didn't wait for him to return."

"Oh, no," Stewart said, pausing as his voice cracked. "I understood there was nothing more I could do. I picked myself up, pulled out the recall module, took a deep breath, and pressed the button."

Kohen saw tears form in Stewart's eyes and allowed a silent moment to pass before asking, "What happened?"

"Nothing happened."

"I beg your pardon?"

"Nothing happened."

"What do you mean nothing happened?"

"The recall module."

"You mean—"

"Yes. I suppose whatever happened in the time jump to cause my wristwatch to malfunction also caused the module to stop working as well. I pressed that button a million times and nothing happened. I was stranded in 1963 with no way back. Not knowing what to do next, I ditched my coveralls, walked to Dealey Plaza, and spent the remainder of that afternoon weeping on the grassy knoll."

"You have no history until shortly before meeting grandma," Kohen said as his hand involuntarily concealed his mouth, "because your history didn't begin until 1963?"

Stewart nodded though the tears. "I had to let go of my other life and create a whole new one. I found work and eventually did well for myself. I met your grandmother in the Spring of 1966 and we got married later that Fall."

"Did she ever know?"

"Yes, she was the only one I ever told, and she kept that secret till the day she died."

"Why didn't you tell anyone else? Why not others in the family?"

"Who would have believed me?"

"Did you ever try to tell anyone about Oswald's innocence?"

"Yes, but not immediately. I was afraid the cops would make the connection to me being the guy outside the basement parking garage the day Oswald was shot, so I waited four years. I contacted the Dallas Police Department to tell them what I knew. Not all of it of course, but just enough to convey the point that Oswald did not kill the president."

"How did that go?"

"Before the week was over I was visited by two men in suits who stood on my doorstep and told me I couldn't have been with Oswald in the lunchroom when the president was shot. They said I had to be mistaken because Oswald was on the sixth floor and he alone shot the president. When I protested, the men told me that if I knew what was best for me, my new bride, and the baby she was carrying, I'd keep my mouth shut. Few people knew she was pregnant at the time. That was enough to convince me to never speak of Oswald's innocence again."

"As much as I want to believe you," Kohen said, "I'm having trouble wrapping my head around all of this."

"I knew you would, that's why I wanted to give you this," Stewart said as he handed Kohen the tattered shoebox.

Kohen didn't waste time asking what was in it. He promptly removed the lid and peered inside. "Is this the—"

"Yes."

"This is remarkable," Kohen said as he took hold of the recall module. "It looks otherworldly."

"Use your fingernail to open the hatch on the rear and slide the switch to unlock it. Then twist the top and bottom portions of the module in opposite directions to open it."

"The circuitry looks quite advanced."

"More than you know. Now remove the circuit board."

Kohen freed the piece with care and held it up for inspection.

"Tell me what you see," Stewart said.

"Made in China?"

"The manufacture date."

Kohen's hand slowly lowered as he turned his gaze toward his grandfather's eyes. "It's dated twenty-one years from now."

Tears began streaming down Stewart's face as he broke under the release of emotions.

Kohen placed his hand on his grandfather's knee as the old man's shoulders heaved.

Minutes passed before Stewart composed himself enough to continue. "I do not believe it is possible for me to exist simultaneously."

"What do you mean?" Kohen asked.

"I am due to be born next year, so I suspect I will have to die soon."

"How long do you have?"

"I will be conceived by the end of this summer, so I will have to be gone before then."

Finding it difficult to summon any words that could possibly bring Stewart comfort, Kohen appealed to the positive: "You lived a good life, grandpa. You did what you could to make the world better and that's more than most men can say."

Stewart was not comforted.

"You've lived a long, healthy, and successful life," Kohen continued. "You did your best and have nothing to regret."

Stewart wept even harder.

"Are you still bothered by not being able to save the president?"

"No. I've come to terms with that failure."

"Then what makes you still this upset after all these years?"

"Because," Stewart stuttered as he retrieved a tissue from the tissue box on the table between them. "I never allowed myself to mourn my own loss."

"Don't beat yourself up over this. I know you sacrificed so much, but you gained a wonderful family. You loved grandma like no one else could have, you raised three boys and two girls who all turned out well, and you have fourteen grandchildren to be proud of."

"It's true, I love my family more than anything, but it came with a cost. I lost something very special."

"What did you lose?"

"My wife."

"Grandma?"

"No. Before I traveled into the past."

"You were previously married?"

26

"Yes, but that's not all. I was a newlywed when I agreed to be the guinea pig in this time travel experiment, and a few months before I was scheduled to depart, I found out my bride and I were expecting a baby. In fact, the day before my trip we found out we were having a girl. We even had a name picked out."

"What was her name?"

"Daphne."

"That's a beautiful name."

"Because of the baby I almost abandoned the mission, but didn't. It's a decision that's always caused me great guilt."

"You were doing something for the greater good of the world. Daphne would've been proud of her father."

"I remember it like it was yesterday. My wife begged me not to go. She was so heartbroken she couldn't bear to watch me drive away. After we said goodbye on the porch she went straight into the house. I imagine her sobbing after I left was second only to when she was told something went terribly wrong with my trip."

"What was *her* name?"

"Tabitha. Beautiful Tabitha. I failed her and my unborn daughter. I left them on that rainy Friday morning and never returned. I always wondered if she ever recovered from the news."

Kohen was robbed of words.

"You're right though," Stewart continued. "I've lived a long, healthy, and successful life, but I've lived every single day of that life haunted that I abandoned my wife and daughter. There are no words to describe that loss and regret."

Kohen grabbed a tissue for himself, then grandfather and grandson stayed up late into the night talking about Stewart's life: past, present, and future.

FIVE

Stewart passed away before summer's end, just as he predicted. The cardiac arrest struck without warning three weeks before Kohen's wedding.

The funeral was much harder on Kohen than he anticipated. Not only because it was held two weeks before he was to marry Stacy, but also because of the secret Stewart passed on to him. Kohen now carried the burden that his grandfather bore his whole life. And, like his grandfather, he had no one to tell.

Kohen waited until the last family member paid their respects before he approached the casket. It was difficult to accept that his grandfather was gone. He could not reconcile the fact that in this crowded room, amidst the varying degrees of pain and loss, time stood still, yet, outside life went on as normal. No one would ever know what his grandfather tried to accomplish for the world, the loss he suffered for it, or the life of regret he endured afterward.

"I know you were haunted by what happened," Kohen said through a stream of tears, "but I have life only because of your loss. And for that, I am forever grateful."

Before returning to his seat beside his fiancé, Kohen reached into his pocket, removed the recall module Stewart gave him several months earlier, and slipped it into the void between his grandfather's chest and folded hands. "Thank you," he said. "I love you."

On May 30th of the following year, with a fresh cup of coffee in hand, Kohen began his morning by scouring the newspaper's birth announcements for babies born the day before. He'd been waiting for this since his grandfather died the previous summer.

It didn't take long for him to find what he was looking for. The third birth notice on the page said that Clarence and Regina Hudson of Dallas welcomed a healthy baby boy into the world at Parkland Hospital. They named him Stewart.

Kohen reclined in his chair with a wide grin as he took a slow sip of his coffee. "Welcome back, grandpa. I missed you."

~~~
## SIX
~~~

Stacy intended to do this from her car, but with nowhere to park on the crowded residential street, she had to park a block away and walk.

Exchanging the climate control and leather seats of her car for an umbrella and a bus bench, she arrived at her destination early in the morning to begin her wait in the rain.

If her husband knew what she was doing that chilly Friday morning he would have come unglued. He'd been reluctant to reveal the secret to her but when he did he was adamant that she never tell anyone. And he warned her countless times over the years, "Never interfere with it, ever!"

Although the bus bench was hard and cold, it was in a perfect location: directly across the street from the house. Not only did it provide Stacy a place to sit, but it also afforded her a cover to not look so conspicuous even though her bright red umbrella screamed, "Take notice of me."

Stacy passed the hours watching small puddles form into larger ones. Several people came and went that morning, sharing the bench with her while they waited for their respective buses. Twice, when a bus arrived and she was the only one there, she waved the driver on.

When Stacy was beginning to wonder if she was at the wrong house, the front door finally opened. She watched as a young couple stepped onto the covered porch and embraced. It wasn't a *see-you-when-you-get-home-after-work* embrace, it was more akin to a *you're-going-away-for-a-long-time* or *you-may-not-make-it-back* embrace.

The man placed his hand on his wife's abdomen and bent slightly as if talking to her stomach. When he was done he gave the woman with swollen red eyes one last kiss. He then turned, opened his umbrella, and descended the porch steps as his wife fled into the house.

Stacy crossed the street and intercepted the man at his car parked beside the curb. "Stewart?" She called out as he was placing his key in the door lock, "Stewart Hudson?"

Startled, the man looked at her for a moment from under his blue umbrella before answering, "Yes."

"I'm Stacy," she said smiling, extending her hand into the curtain of raindrops that separated them.

"I'm terribly sorry but I don't have time to buy anything right now."

"I'm not selling anything," Stacy said, retracting her rejected hand. "I have some important information for you."

"You'll have to come back another time. I'm running late for a trip."

"To 1963?"

Stewart looked to his left and right before leaving the key in the door and taking a step toward her. "What did you just say?"

"If you're headed to 1963, I have some information you will need."

"How do you—"

"Don't ask because I can't tell you."

Stewart lowered his voice, "Who did you say you were again?"

"Stacy."

"Do you have a last name?"

Stacy hesitated.

"What's your last name?"

"Hudson."

Stewart looked surprised. "Are we related?"

"In a roundabout way."

"Look, lady, I don't have time for games. What do you know about my trip?"

"At this point, more than you. That's why I'm here."

A passing car splashed droplets of water onto the legs of Stewart's green coveralls that stuck out below his trench coat.

"Pay careful attention to what I say," Stacy urged. "You'll have your work cut out for you when you get there."

"I'm listening."

"Oswald's not your target—he's not the shooter."

Stewart rolled his eyes. "You can spare me your nutty conspiracy theories."

"And you can spare me your *ad hominem*."

"Look, you have my attention and I'm listening to what you have to say, but I don't subscribe to wild theories."

"I appreciate the enthusiasm by which you cling to your indoctrination, but once you arrive at your destination in about two hours, you will find out the truth. And unless you listen to what I'm telling you right now, you will fail the mission."

"I've studied the assassination and the Kennedy presidency since as far back as I can remember, so you're not going to convince me otherwise."

"You're a smart kid," Stacy said, "but you've still got a lot to learn. Coasting through life by avoiding uncomfortable facts may be a blissful existence for you in many situations but not when it comes to this. There's too much at stake."

"Are you suggesting Oswald had nothing to do with this?"

"No, not nothing, but I can assure you it's not what you've been told your whole life. Now listen, your shooters will be on the depository's sixth floor, in the DalTex building, on the grassy knoll, and who knows how many other locations. In fact, to this day, we still aren't certain about the exact number of shooters or all their locations. What we *do* know is it's a triangulation shooting so you will have to move quickly."

"And exactly how do you know what happened in Dealey Plaza?"

"If you truly want to save Kennedy's life—which is the reason you're risking leaving your wife and daughter without a husband and father—you'll need to trust what I'm telling you."

"How do you know we're having a girl? Even my friends on this project don't know that yet."

"How I know what I know is not important."

"Yes it is. It's vitally important. You're aware of a trip I'm taking that only a handful of people know about, you know about my daughter, which even less people know about, and you're attempting to persuade me from stopping Oswald when I get to my destination. If I ventured a guess I'd say you're here to sabotage my mission."

"I'm trying to prevent your mission from failing, that's why I've contacted you."

"I don't believe it," Stewart said, waving a hand of dismissal before turning to his car and unlocking the door. "I think you're trying to distract me by sending me on a wild goose chase through Dealey Plaza in search of hidden snipers that don't exist."

"You know, Stewart, I would have thought someone who was about to take such a personal risk to save the president would be a little more open minded to the facts surrounding the assassination."

"You'll have to excuse me," he said as he opened the car door, "I must get going."

"Look, Stewart, if I didn't want you to be successful in saving Kennedy's life, I wouldn't be standing here in the rain risking things I don't even understand to ensure you get it right this time!"

Before Stacy could stop them, the words had rolled off her tongue. She cringed on the inside and it showed on her face.

"This time?" Stewart said with one foot in the car. "What do you mean *this time*?"

Stalling to conjure an answer, Stacy cast her gaze at the reflections of their red and blue umbrellas in the puddles.

"You're a time traveler," Stewart said as he stepped toward Stacy, leaving his car door open. "Aren't you?"

Stacy didn't answer.

"That's how you know me. That's how you know we're having a girl."

"I am not a time traveler."

"Then how again is it that you know me and all these details?"

"I think I've said too much already."

"I beg to differ. You haven't said nearly enough."

"Look, I'd rather not say anymore."

"Then tell me who you are."

"I already gave you my name."

"But how do you know me?"

"We've met a couple times and I've been to your funeral once," Stacy said in a failed stab at humor to ease the tension.

Stewart remained stoic.

"I'm married to your grandson," Stacy blurted.

"I knew it. You're a time traveler. You're from the future."

"From the present."

"The present?"

"No, I mean, I'm not a time traveler. I'm from the present."

"How is that possible?"

"I shouldn't say any more. You need to go. You have a mission to accomplish and you're running late. Just remember, once you get there do not focus on Oswald but—"

"Wait a second," Stewart interrupted, thinking out loud. "You're easily more than twice my age, but you say you're married to my grandson and you've been to my funeral. Since I'm only twenty years old, I obviously won't have grandchildren for many years. So you should be from the future, yet you say you're from the present."

Stacy watched as Stewart's mouth opened and his eyes widened. She recognized that he figured it out.

"Something happens to me on my trip, doesn't it?"

36

Stacy was at a loss for what to say but she didn't have to utter a word, he could read it on her face.

"Is everything all right, dear?" a concerned voice beckoned from the porch.

"Yes," Stewart called back to his wife before returning his attention to Stacy and muttering, "I think so."

Stacy wished the woman had stayed in the house. Her heart felt heavy for what Stewart's wife was going through and what she was about to go through, and Stacy knew it didn't help that her husband was talking to a strange woman in the street.

"So what happens to me?" Stewart asked.

"I must go."

"Wait. What happens to me?" Stewart said more forcefully, emphasizing each word.

"You don't . . ." Stacy stuttered before looking over at Stewart's wife.

"I don't what?"

Stacy's eyes remained fixed on the pregnant woman.

"I don't what?"

"You don't come back."

The cadence of raindrops was the only sound shared by Stacy and Stewart as he digested her words.

"Do I get hurt?"

"No."

"Arrested?"

"No."

"Do I end up in the wrong time?"

"No, it's nothing like that."

"So what happens to me?"

"Your module doesn't work."

37

Another brief pause hung in the air between them.

Stewart's wife petitioned again from under the cover of the porch. He didn't respond this time. Instead, he closed and locked his car door.

"What are you doing?" Stacy asked in a panic.

"I'm going to see my wife."

"Your friends are waiting for you at the lab to take this trip."

"I'll call them and let them know I've changed my mind."

"But you can't," Stacy protested. "You have to take this trip."

"A mission I've already failed once? A mission in which you claim there are more assassins than I can reasonably neutralize? And all with the knowledge that I don't return to my wife and unborn child in the process? I may be young and still have a lot to learn, but I'm not crazy."

"But you must go," Stacy pleaded. "You can't abandon your mission."

"I truly appreciate your warning. It has saved my family. Now, if you'll excuse me, I'm going to see my wife." Stewart turned and headed to the porch. "Good day, ma'am."

Stacy remained in the street next to Stewart's car and watched as he embraced his wife again. Not like an *I-missed-you-and-hope-you-had-a-good-day* kind of embrace, but more like a *we-almost-lost-one-another-and-I'm-glad-to-have-a-second-chance-with-you* kind of embrace.

SEVEN

Stacy lost track of how many times she slammed her fists on the steering wheel and screamed within the enclosure of her car.

When she calmed down enough she grabbed her phone to call her husband at work. She had to tell him, she had no choice now.

His cell phone rang unanswered before going to voicemail. Stacy hung up not knowing what to say.

The steering wheel that just took her abuse now became a resting place for her forehead before an audible alert notified her that she received a text message from Kohen. "Sorry," it said. "In a meeting. Can't answer my phone. What's up?"

Sobbing, Stacy used her thumbs to peck the keyboard on the screen. "When is your meeting over?" she typed. "I need to speak with you."

After hitting send, a response arrived a few seconds later. "We are going till 1 when we break for lunch. I will call you then."

"I'm coming there," she texted back. "I'll wait for you in the lobby."

"Is everything ok?"

Stacy paused. Should she just get it out here and now, in such an informal format as a text message, or wait till they were face to face?

Taking too long to answer, another message came in from Kohen that consisted solely of a question mark.

"I'll see you on your lunch break," she replied, then hit send.

EIGHT

Although the clouds still hung low, dark, and ominous, by the time Stacy arrived at Kohen's work there was no longer a need for the windshield wipers.

She found Kohen's car and parked a few stalls from it. Remembering that her phone doesn't receive a signal on the first floor lobby of Kohen's office building, she texted him to let him know she arrived. He acknowledged her in a return text as she walked toward the building.

Normally the dead spot in the lobby irritated Stacy but today she welcomed the lack of a cell signal. She didn't need to be distracted by her phone, she needed to decide what—and how—she was going to tell Kohen, and she only had forty-five agonizing minutes to figure it out before she'd have to face him.

Stacy divided the time sitting, standing, and pacing, but one o'clock didn't sneak up on her. Feeling like an inmate on death row awaiting execution, her attention was tethered to the large clock that hung above the receptionist. The time had come but Stacy still didn't know how she was going to break the news.

At five past the hour she began watching the elevator, but each time the elevator doors opened, her husband did not emerge.

By ten after, Stacy was standing at the elevator.

At a quarter after, she approached the receptionist.

"May I help you?" the young woman asked from behind the wrap-around mahogany desk.

"I'm waiting for my husband who was supposed to be out of his meeting by now. I can't get a signal in here so would you kindly buzz his office to see if he's been delayed?"

"Sure," the girl said with a smile as she began typing into the computer in front of her. "What's the name?"

"Kohen Hudson."

"Who?"

"Kohen Hudson," Stacy repeated.

"Hmm, that doesn't sound familiar, but I've only been here a couple months."

Stacy waited for the receptionist to find what she was looking for on the screen.

"Ma'am," the young girl said, "there is no Kohen Hudson in my directory."

"Well, that's impossible. He's been employed with this company for 16 years. His car is in the parking lot."

"I'm looking at our entire phone database."

"Try again."

The receptionist instead dialed a number. "Hi, Gale, this is Trudy. I have a quick question for you. I have a lady here looking for an employee but I can't find him in the phone bank. Last of Hudson, first of Kohen."

Stacy never took her eyes off the girl.

"Ok. Thank you," Trudy said before hanging up the phone. "I'm sorry, ma'am, that was our human resources department. They confirmed that not only is Kohen Hudson not an employee here, but no one by that name has ever worked here."

Stacy spun on her heel without saying a word. Holding up her phone as she walked through the lobby and out the front door, she kept her eyes focused on the corner of the screen that read *no service*. Once she was in the parking lot she received enough signal strength to make a call and began scrolling through her phone for Kohen's name. It was not there.

Stacy picked up the pace as she walked to her car while pulling up the call screen to dial Kohen directly. She stopped dialing midway through the number when she saw another vehicle parked in the space that Kohen's had occupied when she arrived.

Stacy reached her car by the time her trembling fingers finished typing out Kohen's cell number. Trying to control her breathing, she held the phone to her ear.

"Hello?" a woman's voice answered.

"Who is this?"

"Jennifer. Who is this?"

"I need to speak to Kohen."

"Who?

"Kohen."

"I'm sorry," the voice on the other end of the line said, "you have the wrong number."

"How long have you had this number?"

Stacy's heart raced while Jennifer thought about the question. "About four or five ye—"

Stacy terminated the call amid a flood of tears.

NINE

Stacy's car lost traction on the wet pavement as she sped out of the parking lot. With one hand on the wheel and the other holding her phone, she divided her attention between the road and the screen until she found her best friend's number and hit the call button.

As soon as Amanda answered she could tell Stacy was in tears.

"What's wrong?" Amanda asked.

"I messed up bad."

"What happened? Where are you?"

Stacy stuttered something unintelligible.

"Slow down," Amanda said. "Take a deep breath and collect yourself."

"I think I made a big mistake," Stacy said, "a really big mistake."

"Honey, we've been here for each other since grade school. We've gotten through a lot together and we can get through this too."

"Not this time."

"Just calm down, catch your breath, and tell me what happened."

"There's no fixing this. I've done something terrible."

"What do you mean? What did you do?"

"I think something's happcned to Kohen."

"Who?"

"Kohen," Stacy repeated louder.

"Who's Kohen?"

"My husband," Stacy screamed into the phone.

"What are you talking about? Phillip is your husband."

Stacy looked at her hand on the steering wheel. The wedding ring Kohen gave her had five diamonds inlaid on a gold band. The one she was looking at was a single diamond on a silver band.

"Stacy? Are you there?"

Stacy did not respond.

"Hello?"

Stacy threw her phone onto the passenger seat. The phone bounced off the seat and struck the door. When it came to rest on the floorboard the back of the phone and the battery were lying beside it.

TEN

Slicing through the remaining puddles in the road from the morning's rain, Stacy barely slowed down to make the turn onto her street while inside her chest her heart beat faster. She traveled this route thousands of times over the years but never at this speed.

As Stacy approached her house the first thing that struck her was the color. Her home was sage green with maroon trim when she left this morning, not the dark brown with beige trim she was looking at now. Even the landscaping was different, including the absence of the oak tree in the front yard that Kohen planted after their first child was born.

Stacy careened into the driveway coming to a stop behind two cars she didn't recognize before hopping out. She traversed the walkway to the front door where unfamiliar wooden signs greeted her along the way: *Gone Fishing*, *Two Old Crows Live Here, Life Begins at Retirement*, and *What Happens at Grandma's Stays at Grandma's.*

Above the door hung a hand carved wood sign that read *The Serlings* with an image of a quilt on one side and a fishing rod on the other.

Even though Stacy knew this quasi-familiar place was her house, something inside her compelled her to knock—except it was more like a frantic pounding. It was in this very moment, where she found herself waiting for a stranger to answer her own door, that Stacy realized nothing in her life was going to be the same.

The door was answered by an elderly gentleman who stood silent as Stacy assaulted him with a salvo of questions. "Who are you? What are you doing in my house?" Stacy even demanded to know the answer to a question she wasn't sure she understood herself: "And where's my husband?"

The old man did not answer Stacy, but he did answer his wife who asked if she should call the police. "Yes, dear," he said. "Please do."

"What did you do to my house?" Stacy continued without waiting for an answer, before declaring, "You don't belong here."

"Look, ma'am, I think you've made a mistake," the old man said. "Perhaps you're on the wrong street."

"This is my home. My husband and I moved here after we married. We raised our kids in this hou—"

The old man watched Stacy's face change from distress and anger to fear and shock as she cut her words short before bolting back to her car.

Stacy flung the passenger door open and sat on the seat. With her feet still planted on the driveway, she retrieved her phone from the floorboard.

"The cops are on their way," the old man's wife said when she joined him at the front door.

The elderly couple kept an eye on Stacy as she fumbled with the battery, seating it back into her phone, and not bothering to replace the cover.

Stacy waited the eternity it took for the phone to power on before entering her passcode. Through the blur of tear-filled eyes Stacy dialed a number and waited.

"This is Stacy Hudson," she said into the phone after the person on the other end answered, "Sutterfield University, how can I help you?"

"I am Josiah Hudson and Caroline Hudson's mother," Stacy said. "We have a family emergency. I need to speak with Josiah and Caroline immediately."

After a few minutes the voice on the other end of the phone informed her that there were no students by those names enrolled at that college.

Stacy crumpled to the ground sobbing. The older couple slowly closed their door as the sound of a distant siren grew louder.

ELEVEN

The trio exchanged hugs and good-byes. Silhouetted by their porch light, Stewart and Tabitha watched as the old woman ambled to her car and drove into the night.

The couple entered their living room where their daughter was wide awake sitting on the couch between her two younger brothers who—succumbing to bellies full of turkey, potatoes, stuffing, and pumpkin pie— were sprawled on both sides of her.

"Mom and dad, can I ask you a question?"

"Sure, honey," Stewart said.

"Why does Stacy spend—"

"Manners," Stewart interrupted.

"Sorry, dad," Daphne said. "Why does Ms. Stacy spend every Thanksgiving with us."

Stewart and Tabitha cast a glance at one another, knowing this subject was going to be broached one day. "I'll get the boys to bed," Tabitha said, calling dibs before Stewart.

After his wife scooped up one of the boys, Stewart took a seat next to his daughter in the newly vacated spot.

"Do you like Ms. Stacy?" Stewart asked his daughter.

"Oh, yes. She's a very nice lady. I was just wondering why she spends Thanksgiving with us every year. Doesn't she have a family of her own?"

Stewart thought for a moment before continuing. "You know how I work on time travel at the lab?"

"Yes, and how I'm not supposed to talk about time trips to anyone."

"To be more precise, Daphne, the research and testing of time travel are common knowledge to the public, it's the specifics of any particular time trip that we're not to discuss with anyone."

"I understand, but what does that have to do with Ms. Stacy?"

"Well, when you were just an itty bitty peanut in your mommy's tummy, your daddy was going to travel back in time. It was during the early stages of our experimentation and it was going to be my first trip."

"Where to?" Daphne asked excitedly.

"Places, dates, and times are all specifics," Stewart said, casting a sideways glance.

"Right, dad."

"Anyway, on that time trip I wasn't going to come back."

"Why didn't you want to come back?"

"Oh, I wanted to come back, but a malfunction in the recall module was going to prevent me from doing so."

"I don't understand."

"If I went on that trip I wouldn't have been able to return. Your mommy would have lost her husband, you would have grown up without your daddy, and your little brothers wouldn't be here."

"Why didn't you just fix it before going on the trip?"

"Because the module was going to malfunction during the trip. There would have been no way to know that until it was too late. And to this day, we still don't know why it would have failed."

"But if you never time tripped, how did you know it wasn't going to work?"

"Excellent question. That's where Ms. Stacy comes in."

"Oh, this should be good."

"It is," Stewart chuckled. "You see, Ms. Stacy knew what was going to happen if I traveled back in time, so on the morning of my trip she stopped me on my way to the lab."

"She came to warn you?"

"Well, not exactly. She had advice for me for the trip, but she inadvertently informed me that I wouldn't return if I went."

"That was a good thing, right?"

"Yes. But warning me wasn't her intention, and, unfortunately for Ms. Stacy, it cost her severely."

"What do you mean?"

"By not taking that trip, Ms. Stacy's life was turned upside down."

"But if you went, then *our* lives would have been turned upside down."

"Exactly."

"I think I understand," Daphne said, clinging to her father's every word. "But how did this affect Ms. Stacy?"

"Because Ms. Stacy's life, as she knew it, was intricately woven into the actions I would have taken had I gone on that trip. By choosing to stay, I altered her whole world."

Tabitha returned to take the remaining brother. With his smooshed cheek resting in the crook of her arm, his cradled body stayed limp as Tabitha carried him to his bedroom.

"Something doesn't make sense," Daphne said.

"What's that, sunshine?"

"How did Ms. Stacy know you were going to go on a time trip that morning? I thought places, dates, and times were all kept secret."

"She's a perceptive kid," Tabitha said as she disappeared down the hall while a line of drool from the boy's mouth made its way to her elbow.

"And," Daphne added, "how did Ms. Stacy know the module wasn't going to work?"

"I don't know how to tell you this," Stewart said before pausing to gaze at the ceiling as he searched, not for the words to say, but how to say them.

"Just say it."

"It's very complicated."

"But I'm very smart, dad," Daphne said, looking up at Stewart from under his arm.

"I planned on telling you about this one day, but I always envisioned you being much older."

"I may only be twelve, but I can handle it. You heard mom. I'm perspective."

"Perceptive."

"That too."

"You have to promise me you will never breathe a word of this to anyone."

"Not even to my brothers?"

"Your mother and I will tell them when they're older."

"Promise," Daphne said extending a curved pinky finger.

The two sealed the deal with a pinky promise before Stewart drew a deep breath. "Truth is, I *did* travel back in time. Long before even Ms. Stacy was born. And I got stuck there."

"Then how are you here? And how did you meet Ms. Stacy?"

Stewart again found himself searching for words. "I suppose I should come right out and say it. Ms. Stacy married my grandson."

Daphne's deeply furrowed eyebrows revealed she was not only confused, but was on the verge of respectfully calling her dad crazy. She opted for a nicer expression of disbelief: "That makes no sense. How is that even possible? You have no grandkids and she's way older than you."

"This is where it gets complicated, sweetheart."

"I'm all ears."

"When I got stuck in the year I traveled to I eventually married and had a family."

Daphne's look of confusion increased.

"You're not getting the sordid details so don't bother asking," Stewart added. "Eventually I became a grandpa to a smart and handsome young man named Kohen. And then Kohen married Stacy, who became my granddaughter-in-law. And she is the one who stopped me on the way to the lab."

"The same Stacy that visits us every Thanksgiving?"

"Yes."

"So, why did she stop you on the morning of your trip?"

"According to Ms. Stacy, when I traveled back in time I failed my mission. So, Ms. Stacy met with me to give me information to ensure I accomplished what I was intending to do. But while telling me these things, she let it slip that I wouldn't be returning from my trip. With that information, I chose not to go."

"What was your mission?"

"Specifics, Daphne."

"Right, dad. But I still don't see how this affected Ms. Stacy."

"Since I didn't go back in time I didn't get stuck there. Since I didn't get stuck there, I didn't get married and have a family there. So Kohen was never born which means Stacy never married him. Stacy's entire life with Kohen ceased to exist when I chose not to travel back in time."

"This is hurting my head."

"After this happened Stacy had a hard time adjusting to a life she was unfamiliar with. In a split second she lost Kohen and the two children they had together, and in turn, gained a new husband and four kids she didn't know and had no recollection of."

"How did her family deal with it?"

"Not well. Everyone thought she went crazy and within a year's time her husband left her."

"What about her kids?"

"They've all grown up and moved away. They still keep in touch, but as you can imagine, their relationships with her were never the same."

"That's so awful."

"Because of all Ms. Stacy went through, your mother and I stayed in touch with her. We were the only ones she could talk to because we were the only ones who knew what had happened."

"So you and mom became like family to her?"

"You can say that. And since it was Thanksgiving time when her world came crashing down, you can

53

imagine how painful and lonely this time of the year is for her. The following year we offered for Ms. Stacy to spend the holiday with us and to our delight she's come over every year since. Her first Thanksgiving with us was also our first Thanksgiving with you. And if it wasn't for Ms. Stacy's sacrifice, we wouldn't be sitting together here today."

"That's an amazing story, dad."

"What do you say we have some of that leftover pie?"

"But you guys never let me eat sweets this late."

"I'll make an exception."

"Deal."

Not bothering to use plates, father and daughter sat down at the table in front of a half eaten pumpkin pie.

After just one bite, Daphne put her fork down and sat on Stewart's lap. "I'm so glad you stayed," she said as she hugged him with her face buried in his neck. "If you never came back I would have lost the best daddy in the world."

Tabitha walked in, stopping at the entry to the kitchen. Smiling, she watched without saying a word.

"I'm so glad I stayed too," Stewart said, catching a glimpse of his wife over Daphne's shoulder.

"And I'm so thankful for what Ms. Stacy did," Daphne said. "Thanksgiving means so much more to me now."

Tabitha walked over and wrapped her arms around her husband and daughter, hugging them tightly before putting a kettle of water on the stove. The three of them stayed up late that night eating pumpkin pie, drinking hot tea, and enjoying each other's company.

The End.

The Visitor

J.L. Pattison

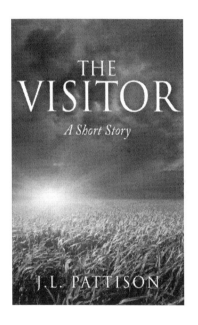

The Visitor

J.L. Pattison

Elroy Jenkins was startled from his afternoon nap when his dog launched itself off the back porch and disappeared into the cornfield.

Rising from his chair, Elroy rubbed the sleep from his eyes and ambled down the steps.

Following the sound of Monroe's uncharacteristic barking, he entered the towering rows of stalks expecting to find the dog confronting an unwelcome critter. But when he located Monroe he saw that his faithful companion was barking and growling at something in the sky. Elroy glanced upward as he approached, but saw nothing.

Attempting to calm Monroe, Elroy knelt down to take hold of the manic hound when a blinding flash of light, accompanied by a jolting pop, sent Monroe yelping away with his tail between his legs.

Elroy stood and spun around to see a man standing just a few feet away. The rich soil between the rows of corn softened Elroy's fall as he stumbled over his own feet.

The stranger—dressed in clothes unfamiliar to Elroy—was shielding his face with his hands.

Seconds passed, which felt more like minutes, before the man finally exhaled and dropped his hands.

Elroy remained reclined on his elbows in the dirt, too afraid to move.

The stranger's eyelids cracked to a hesitant squint before shooting wide open. Throwing his head from left to right, he surveyed his surroundings.

When the man finally saw Elroy lying on the ground, he recoiled. Elroy reciprocated by scooting backward.

"Where am I?" the man asked Elroy.

Elroy remained motionless and did not answer.

"Is this Philadelphia?" the man asked.

Elroy sat up but kept silent, never taking his eyes off the stranger.

"Answer me! Am I in Philadelphia? Is this 1775?"

Seeing the panic in the man's eyes, Elroy broke his silence. "No, sir," he said with a cracked voice. "It's 1899, and you're in Georgia, standing in my cornfield."

~~~
ONE
~~~

Theodore Garfield used his monogrammed handkerchief to wipe the sweat from his forehead and neck. Under the shade of the soaring Georgia pines, Elroy's front porch couldn't hold back the searing heat of the June 1946 afternoon. Even the occasional breeze was inadequate at nudging the bugs, let alone circulating the stagnant, humid air.

"Well, Mr. Jenkins," Theodore said as he placed his empty jar on the splintered table that sat between the two men. "I've truly appreciated your time and hospitality this afternoon, and especially your delicious sweet tea."

"And I appreciated the company, young man. It's not often that I get visitors, and especially no one famous."

"I would hardly define myself as famous," Theodore said, brandishing a smile, "although I hope to be one day."

"Your articles in the Tribune get read by everyone in this county, don't they?"

"Yes."

"See, you're already famous. It's all a matter of perspective. Very few people know of me, but many people know Theodore Garfield because of the articles you write."

"Well, I won't be truly happy till I am read all over the state, and then the country. And that will not happen if I remain here writing for this paper. I expect to move on one day and work for a big newspaper; you

58

know, like in the city. And I see nothing stopping me. I'm pretty good at what I do. That's why I'm the youngest writer to ever work for the Tribune."

"That's quite an accomplishment."

"And after my article hits the papers tomorrow, everyone in this county will know who Elroy Jenkins is."

"What page will it be on?"

"I've been told that your story will run on the front page. It's not every day someone in our county reaches their centennial birthday. That is quite a news story for this part of Georgia—especially a former slave like yourself." Theodore tucked his drenched handkerchief into his pocket. "Before I go, do you have any secrets to your longevity that you'd like to share with our readers?"

"A joyful heart leads to a long life," Elroy said without hesitation. "Never cease to be thankful and always be content in every situation. Every day that you wake up and get out of bed, you should be grateful to the good Lord for granting you another day that you don't deserve."

"That is good," Theodore said as he scribbled onto his notepad.

"And when you celebrate your 100th birthday—"

"Whoa, not so fast," Theodore said, laughing from behind his held-up hand. "I still have seventy-eight years to go to reach that milestone, and with my family history, I'd be fortunate if I made fifty. My daddy, my granddaddy, and both my uncles all died before their fiftieth birthdays. I reckon if I can live long enough to see fifty, I'll have received more than I expected."

"That's true. And even if you were to die tomorrow, you should still be thankful for the twenty-two years that God has already granted you."

"I see wisdom comes with age. Tell me, do you have any words of advice from a century of living?"

"Well, whether you become the president, write for a big city paper, or just raise corn, live each day as if it's your last. If you do that, not only will you always remain humble, but even the roses you rush past every day will look more stunning, their scent will be more beautiful, and their thorns won't be such an inconvenience. The man who expects to live a hundred years never takes the time to behold a rose because he tells himself that he doesn't have time for that now; he'll just get to that another day. The man who doesn't expect tomorrow cherishes all that he has today, even the trials."

Theodore leaned back in his chair thinking about the advice. "You've lived a long life, Mr. Jenkins. Do you have any regrets?"

Elroy stopped rocking his chair and gazed at the weathered floorboards beneath his feet. "Would your newspaper ever run a story," Elroy said, still looking down, "on a strange event that happened many years ago on this very farm?"

"Well," Theodore answered, "I imagine so, as long as it met certain criteria."

"Like what?"

"Well, first of all, my editor has to approve all stories before printing. Secondly, it would have to be a true fact—no rumor or unsubstantiated gossip. And thirdly, it would have to be newsworthy."

"Like a local resident turning 100?"

"Right. It would have to interest our readers. And my editor loves local stories, because our readers love local stories."

"Like Mrs. Carver winning that award last year for her peach pie?"

"Yes, exactly like that."

"That was a very well written article, by the way." Elroy's eyes met Theodore's. "The way you described that pie, I could almost taste it."

"Thank you. It was one of the first stories I wrote for the paper when I got hired, and I can attest, that pie was truly worth reporting on. So, tell me, what's this strange story you have in mind?"

Elroy took a deep breath. "Can you spare me another hour of your time?"

Theodore consulted his watch, then glanced at the Spanish moss that hung from the mighty oak branches above his Packard Clipper in the driveway.

"Will it be worth my time?"

"Oh, I think so."

"I can give you thirty minutes."

"Agreed," Elroy said grabbing his cane that rested against the table and using it to raise himself. "Allow me a few minutes to retrieve something from inside."

"All right, but then you'll only have twenty-five minutes remaining."

"What if I redeemed that five minutes by bringing you another glass of tea when I return?"

"Do you have any more ice?"

"A little, yes."

"Deal."

Elroy grabbed Theodore's empty glass and, supporting himself on the cane with the other hand, disappeared behind the screen door. The young reporter swatted at a cloud of gnats with his pencil before securing it behind his ear and closing his notepad.

A few minutes later, Elroy emerged and placed the jar of tea on the table. Theodore didn't wait for the three chunks of jagged ice to stop dancing in the amber liquid before placing the glass to his parched lips.

Elroy took his seat and removed an envelope from his shirt pocket. He laid it on the table in front of Theodore and rested both hands on the crook of his cane.

Theodore reached for the envelope.

"Be patient," Elroy said. "Before you read the letter inside, let me tell you how I came to possess it." Theodore pulled his hand back. "You may want to get your notepad and pencil ready," Elroy instructed. "I am about to tell you the story of a lifetime."

TWO

When Theodore finished reading the letter, he placed it on the table and, raising the upturned Mason jar skyward, quenched himself with the last of the sweet tea.

"So what you're telling me," Theodore said as he placed the empty glass next to the letter, "is that some man from the future tried to use a time machine to visit this nation's founding fathers a year before they signed the Declaration of Independence so he could warn them of what their country would eventually become?"

"Yes sir. The machine not only transported a person through time, but also to specific locations."

"And, by accident, this time traveler missed his intended time and place and ended up in your corn field in 1899?"

"Uh huh," Elroy said nodding.

"And this letter, chronicling major historical events from the eighteenth century to the twenty-first century, was supposed to be given to men like Benjamin Franklin and Thomas Jefferson?"

"That's right."

"There's a problem with your story."

"Oh, yeah?"

"Why did this time traveler . . ." Theodore paused as he looked for the signatory's name on the letter, ". . . this Eric Blair fellow, give the letter to *you*? Realizing his mistake, why didn't he just travel further back in time to give the letter to those he intended?"

63

"He would not have a second chance to use the machine. It belonged to his boss who was some sort of scientist who strictly forbade the machine to be used to go back in time because he did not want history altered."

"But the guy used the machine anyway?"

"Mr. Blair's conscience would not allow him to rest knowing he had the means to change history for the better. So when his boss was not around, he seized the opportunity to sound the alarm, risking his life in the process. If things went well, he would be out of a job when he returned but history would be much improved and countless lives saved. If things didn't go as planned, he could have died or been lost in time somewhere. Something obviously went wrong; that's how he ended up in my cornfield and I ended up with his letter."

"Were there any witnesses of his visit?"

"Just me."

"What about the hired hands who worked for you? Surely someone tending your fields would have seen him."

"Unfortunately, Mr. Blair arrived on a Sunday and my help never worked on Sundays."

"What about your wife?"

"After my wife and I returned home from church earlier that day, I was resting on the back porch when the man showed up, but my wife was in her room taking a nap. That was during the time she was suffering daily from the illness that took her life the following year."

"Did you ever tell her about the visitor?"

"Does a coonhound hunt? Of course I told her. Right after that man vanished mid-sentence, I ran to the house and woke her up."

"And? Did she believe your story?"

"Not at first. She, like you, thought I was crazy. It took her several weeks, or maybe it was a month or two, before she finally believed me. Unfortunately, I think a part of her always remained skeptical. If only she had lived long enough to see the events the letter predicted after the turn of the century, then I'm certain she would have believed."

"Did you tell anyone else?"

"Oh, sure. I told a lot of people."

"And showed them the letter?"

"Yes."

"And how did that go?"

"Not well. Nobody believed me."

"But the letter mentioned the Titanic tragedy in 1912. If what you're telling me is true, wouldn't someone have believed you when that happened?"

"After enduring ridicule from those I told, and due to my wife's ailing health, I stopped telling the story and stopped showing the letter. After she died I packed the letter away. It was over a decade later that the Titanic sank. No one remembered the details of the letter that I showed them all those years earlier, but I remembered. And I remembered the letter mentioning a world war breaking out within a couple years of the ship's sinking. So I began looking for the letter." Elroy bowed his head while trying to find the words to continue. "But I couldn't find it."

"You lost it?"

"I misplaced it."

"When did you find it again?"

"Last September."

"Just after World War II ended?"

"A few months after, yes."

"Let me get this straight," Theodore said smirking while shooing a persistent fly away from his face. "During the years this letter's validity could have been proven, it went missing, only to reappear after those events passed?"

"I'm afraid so. You see, I believe God is sovereign, and if man develops a way to travel through time to change the outcome of certain past events—events that God has ordained to take place—then no matter what we do, we will not be able to change them. This could explain Mr. Blair showing up at the wrong time and place, and how I misplaced the letter for over forty years."

"Even if you hadn't lost the letter, do you honestly think you could have prevented either World War?"

"No . . . no I don't."

"And the next major event your letter predicts is," Theodore picked up the letter and scanned it, "the assassination of an American president in 1963?"

"Yes, sir."

"Is that the coup d'etat you said Mr. Blair was referring to?"

"It is."

"Now we have to wait almost two decades for the next prediction to corroborate your story. How convenient."

"I'm too old, but you have seventeen years to stop the next event from happening."

"But you said God is in control of everything, so why are you wasting your time?"

"God's sovereignty over the affairs of man does not mean we are exempt of our responsibility to do good. I would still warn you if a tree were to begin falling toward you."

"Mr. Jenkins, I must say, this is all quite shocking."

"I assure you, Mr. Blair's appearance in my cornfield was quite a shock to the both of us too."

"No, sir, I mean this whole tale is shocking. You'll have to forgive me but I simply do not believe any of this," Theodore said as he wiped beads of sweat from his forehead.

"I understand. If I were you I'd find my story difficult to believe as well, but I promise you, this really happened. And I wouldn't have believed the contents of the letter myself had it not been given to me by the stranger who appeared out of nowhere, and then an hour later, vanished before my eyes."

"Returning to the future?" Theodore snickered.

"Presumably."

"You know, Mr. Jenkins, I'm not sure which is more absurd: your story about how you got this letter, or the letter itself. These predictions are downright laughable."

"To you and me these are predictions about a future we cannot conceive of, but to Mr. Blair, they're his history."

"Nonsense. Those events will never happen."

"How do you know that?"

"Because we are not depraved barbarians, we are a civilized, churchgoing society."

"Need I remind you that we just came out of a war where a whole country of civilized, churchgoing Germans either participated *in*, or turned a blind eye *to*, the most horrific treatment of their fellow man?"

"That is different. We are Americans and we would never tolerate what happened in Germany to happen in this country."

"*This country*? Have you forgotten the cruelty that my people and I suffered—and still suffer—at the hands of those in *this country*?"

"We learn from our mistakes. Americans would never participate in the things this letter claims; we would never permit it."

"If there's one thing I've learned in my long life, it's that whether it's the slave ships of America or the death camps of Germany, people are alike all over. Given the right circumstances, good and moral people are capable of great atrocities."

"Come on, Mr. Jenkins," Theodore said shaking his head, "I've heard enough. There is no such thing as time travel, and whoever wrote this letter is a raving mad man. Furthermore, you have nothing to corroborate your tale. You lost the letter during the years it could have proved your story—only to miraculously find it again after all those events passed—and now we have to wait until you're long gone for the next event in the letter to happen." Theodore realized his tone was impolite, but continued without apology. "No rational person would ever believe any of this, and to be quite honest with you, I am offended that you would offer this tall tale to me as a legitimate idea to run in the paper. I am going to be a respected journalist, not some crackpot contributor for a tabloid."

Theodore stood as he placed his pad and pencil in his shirt pocket. "Thank you for your time, Mr. Jenkins, and for the tea, but I must go now."

"Take the letter."

68

"I beg your pardon?"

"Take the letter."

"Listen, Mr. Jenkins, I've humored you long enough. I am not interested in this story or your letter."

"Please, Theodore, take the letter."

Theodore hesitated for a moment before producing a coin from his pocket and tossing it on the table. When it came to rest he said, "This coin bears the motto, 'In God We Trust.' You will never persuade me to believe that the utter depravity of our society described in this letter will ever happen in this great nation of ours, including the absurd notion that our own government would ever be involved in the murder of one of our own presidents."

"At least take the letter and put it away till the next event is predicted to occur. If nothing happens you can discard the letter and forget all about this. What will it hurt?"

"I do not have the inclination, nor patience, to wait that long to prove you wrong."

"Believe me, seventeen years will pass quicker than you think."

The young reporter looked at the letter on the table trying to think of another way to decline Elroy's offer, but nothing came to him. Theodore snatched the letter and tucked it in his pocket. "It was a pleasure to have made your acquaintance," he said. "Good day, sir."

The steps of the old porch creaked when Theodore descended them. He crossed the yard to his car, scattering the chickens in the driveway as he drove off.

Once Theodore returned to his office, he began working on the story that would appear in the following day's paper. He told of Elroy's life before and after slavery, including Elroy's strong faith which led him to forgive his former slaveholders. The article spoke of how Elroy was self-educated and exceptionally smart. It detailed how, in spite of difficult beginnings, Elroy worked hard enough to purchase his own farm and make an above-standard living. The article concluded with Elroy's advice on living a long life, and a mention of the old man's delicious sweet tea.

As Theodore typed, the letter lay in the trash next to his desk among paper coffee cups and crumpled balls of discarded rough drafts.

THREE

Theodore didn't ring in the New Year with the rest of the world. Unable to sleep, he stared at the ceiling above his bed just as he did every night in his apartment since receiving the diagnosis.

Cancer was what the doctor said—irreversible, inoperable cancer.

Theodore never saw it coming. He expected to die of heart failure before his fiftieth birthday like the other men in his family. He did not expect to die of cancer just before his fortieth.

Since receiving the news in mid-December, Theodore spent the final two weeks of 1962 taking stock of his life. From his humble beginnings working at his hometown newspaper, to his position at one of Atlanta's largest papers, it had been a long road, none of which mattered anymore. The thirty-eight-year-old bachelor would never know the devotion and love of a wife, nor experience the joy of little ones jumping on his bed to wake him with bear hugs and little kisses, sticky with pancake syrup.

Theodore always wanted to settle down and have a family, but his voracious appetite for success left no time for that. His whole life was a blur, having spent it all as if he were in a race. A race for recognition, the next news lead, the next promotion, and the next big thing that tomorrow would bring.

Standing at the precipice of death, Theodore now feared all tomorrows, for each day that passed brought him closer to the end, and for the first time in his life, he wanted the days to stop . . . or at least slow down.

~~~
# FOUR
~~~


Quade Harrison enjoyed the crisp November air as he drove across the city. He pulled into the hospital parking lot just before lunchtime with his mind on everything he still had to do at the office. Quade hadn't factored in a hospital visit today, but a call from Theodore's nurse changed his plans.

When Quade arrived at Room 101, he found Theodore exactly as he was during last week's visit, except this time Quade barely recognized his former coworker whose body now heaved with every breath he took.

"Theo," Quade whispered into the still room. After getting no response he stepped closer and called his name again. Opening his eyes, Theodore cast his gaze toward Quade before mustering a partial smile.

"I'm here," Quade said in a hushed tone as he placed his hand on Theodore's arm.

"Thank you for coming," said Theodore, pushing the words out though the pain. "Please have a seat."

Quade located the only chair in the room and slid it across the tile floor. The metal legs emitted a screech that made Theodore's diminutive frame tense.

"Sorry," Quade said while taking a seat next to the bed. "How are you doing?"

"I could complain, but it wouldn't change anything."

"Your nurse said you needed to speak with me. She told me it was urgent."

"We worked together for several years," Theodore said.

"Four, yes."

"Of everyone I'm acquainted with, you're the only one I can speak to about this. You will be the only soul I have ever told this to. I just ask that you hear me out before coming to any conclusions."

"Sure," Quade said as he shifted in the uncomfortable chair.

Theodore became quiet. He gathered his thoughts while staring out the window watching golden leaves liberate themselves from barren tree branches.

In the silence of the room Quade sat patiently—almost reverently—pondering his own mortality while waiting for Theodore to speak.

FIVE

Out of respect for his dying friend, Quade tried to hide the look of disbelief on his face while simultaneously feigning interest in Theodore's story about Elroy Jenkins. "So, what was in the letter?" he asked.

"Warnings about the future of America and the world," Theodore said. "When I met Elroy, World War II had recently ended and the next event mentioned in the letter was still a ways off, so I had no way to corroborate its contents."

"What was the next event?"

"The assassination of an American president less than twenty years after World War II."

"The war ended in 1945," Quade said out loud as he did the math in his head. "That was seventeen years ago."

"Yes," said Theodore, "we're quickly approaching twenty years. It's been so long since I viewed the letter that I can't remember the date it's supposed to happen—not even the year. But for some reason I've never forgotten the president's name."

"The letter actually revealed the name of the president who's supposed to be assassinated?"

"Yes."

"Who?"

"Kennedy."

"Our current president?"

"Yes."

"Oh, come on," Quade said. "You're one of the smartest men I know, and the one I respected the most at the paper. This is obviously just your medication speaking."

"You promised to hear me out."

Quade acquiesced with a nod and Theodore continued. "It wasn't until 1952 that I first heard of Kennedy, when he was elected to the senate. At that time I still didn't believe the contents of the letter, but I'd be lying if I said I didn't entertain the thought that perhaps Elroy was right and the letter was true. But I dismissed it all as coincidence. I mean, what were the odds that this newly elected senator would actually become president of the United States? Then, in 1960, he announced his intention to run for president. It made my blood run cold. Needless to say, after that announcement I began watching Kennedy's political career very closely."

"And when he was elected president?"

"That's when I believed Elroy. That letter could not have been a hoax. When I interviewed him in 1946, there's no way he could have known about the future President. That alone validates the letter for me."

"So, did the letter mention where the assassination is supposed to take place?" Quade asked with raised brow.

"I don't remember the exact city, just the state."

"Surely, if you believe this stuff you would have remembered the details, no?"

"I only read the letter once. Since I did not believe what I was reading at the time I had no reason to commit it to memory. Oh, how I've racked my brain over the years trying to remember the details. Please believe me when I tell you that the president's life is in danger. You must do whatever you can to stop it from happening. His murder will profoundly affect this nation. America will never be the same after that day."

"You said you remember the state the president is to be assassinated in?"

"Yes." Theodore said grimacing as he shifted his body to seek comfort. "Texas."

Quade's eyes grew large. "President Kennedy is campaigning for reelection in Texas right now. He is headed to Dallas from Fort Worth this morning. In fact," Quade said while looking at his watch, "he should be arriving in Dallas as we speak." Quade caught himself and shook his head. "But President Kennedy has been to Texas many times. There's nothing to be alarmed about regarding this visit. Besides, assassinations of presidents no longer happen. That's the stuff of history books. Our presidents are well protected from that sort of thing nowadays."

"Not if the assassins are on the inside—"

The men were interrupted when the door opened. "Excuse me, gentlemen, I hate to bother you, but I need two minutes," the nurse said before turning her attention to Theodore. "It's time for your medication."

"Julia, I told you I don't want any meds until I am done speaking with my friend. I need clarity of mind."

"The doctor allowed you to skip your morning medication so you could visit with your guest, but he was adamant that you not skip two in a row."

"I still need a little more time."

"Sorry, honey, I'm just following the doctor's orders."

Quade watched as Julia placed a pill into Theodore's mouth and followed it with a sip of water before leaving the room.

"Kennedy was elected president almost four years ago," Quade said as soon as the door closed. "Why have you waited until now to tell someone?"

Theodore raised his face toward the ceiling and closed his eyes. Quade listened to the cadence of Theodore's labored breathing while waiting for an answer. "I am ashamed to admit it, but I was in fear that if I told someone, it would've done irreparable harm to my career. Even after receiving the news that I had about a year to live, my dogged arrogance still convinced me to remain quiet to not risk tarnishing my legacy after I died. I have been such a fool and this is the capstone of my life of vanity."

"Don't be so hard on yourself," Quade said while retrieving a wet sponge from the nightstand to moisten Theodore's lips.

"I used to turn the pages of my calendar month after month, year after year, without thinking twice about it," Theodore said, "but this past year it has crushed me every time I turned those pages. It meant that I was getting closer to the end. And when a man lives with that degree of weight on his shoulders, it has a way of changing him." Tears began following the creased channels of Theodore's sunken face. "Now I have bigger concerns. The Bible says it's a terrifying thing to fall into the hands of the living God, and I'm facing that now. I'm so afraid to die."

"Whatever became of Elroy?" Quade asked, attempting to change the subject.

78

"If my memory serves me correct, he died a year or two after I interviewed him. How I'd give anything to talk to him again."

"And where's the letter now?"

"Long gone. I disposed of it the same day Elroy gave it to me."

Quade glanced at his watch. "Listen, Theo, I must get back to work. I still have much to accomplish today."

"Please. Just give me a few more minutes. That's about all the time of coherency I have until the medication takes over. I have so much more to tell you."

"How about another time, Theo? I plan on returning next week."

"I don't know how much time I have left. I need to tell you what else is coming."

Judging by the occasional slurring of Theodore's words, Quade obliged him an extra few minutes, expecting the medication to soon put an end to the conversation.

SIX

"World War II was the last war this country will ever engage in where our freedoms were actually in jeopardy," Theodore said with renewed fervor. He was invigorated with the second wind of a dying man desperate to deliver a warning, and whose only adversary was the clock.

"So there will be no more wars?" Quade asked.

"Oh, no. There will be plenty of wars. The letter listed one conflict after another, ad nauseum, but none of the coming wars will have anything to do with defending our country, including the one we're currently fighting in Vietnam."

"But communism—"

"Will be a greater threat from within than from any foreign country," Theodore interrupted.

"I don't understand. Why would we go to war if not to defend ourselves?"

"Profit."

"Come on, Theo. No president would ever sacrifice our soldiers for monetary gain. And the American people would never send their young men to die for money."

"The people will be told the wars are necessary to defend their freedoms."

"The people would rebel before that."

"Not if the wars are all fought overseas. As long as they're happening far away, you'd be amazed at what we'll tolerate when we reach the apex of apathy."

"Surely we would grow tired of war."

"No, the people will demand more wars once they are convinced that war is peace."

"We're not that naïve."

"Maybe not right now, but soon people's ability to reason—even their desire for truth itself—will wane, eventually being replaced with only a thirst for *panem et circenses*, like in the days of Rome."

"*Panem et circenses*?"

"Bread and circuses," Theodore answered. "As long as the people are fed and entertained, they will care about little else."

"America is not Rome."

"Not yet. Elroy said that, within the next couple generations, Americans will become so distracted by various gratifications that they won't even realize their government revoked most of their liberties. And by the time they recognize what's happening, it will be too late. They'll awaken to discover that they've amused themselves to death."

"There would be resistance."

"There will be no resistance to the boot on their necks. And eventually they will grow to love the boot." Theodore paused as he struggled to swallow before continuing. "Do you remember President Eisenhower's farewell address?"

"Of course, I covered it for the paper almost three years ago."

"What was that entity he warned the American people to beware of?"

"The military-industrial complex?"

"That's it. Don't you think it's odd that he would caution us about such a thing in his farewell address?"

81

"Sure, but I don't see what that has to do with all these other things you're telling me about."

"It has everything to do with what I'm telling you about."

"I'm sorry, Theo, but I stand by my conviction that the people of this nation would never allow their government to go to war without provocation."

"Ah, but if the provocation is manufactured—"

"Mark my words," Quade interrupted, "these things will never happen in America."

"Your argument of incredulity does not make the reality of what I'm telling you any less true."

"So why are you telling me all of this? What do you expect me to do?"

"I'm telling you because I don't want to take this to my grave and you're the only person I can trust. I am not sure how much of a difference you can make, but I know you can do more than I can now. I implore you to do whatever you can to prevent Kennedy's assassination because once that happens, everything will change."

Quade checked his watch again as he conceded that further debate was useless. He reasoned to himself that the man who had succumbed to such delusions would shortly succumb to the narcotics. He counted the seconds.

No longer able to keep his eyes open, Theodore struggled through the advancing lethargy to tell Quade that corruption will become the standard in commerce, politics, and society; that obscenity in behavior and speech will saturate everything from magazines and movies to newspapers and churches; and that every vice and deviancy man could think up will be embraced, legalized, and celebrated.

Theodore spoke of a future where their government would engage in surveilling its own citizens—cataloguing their every move, action, and thought—all under the guise of keeping them safe. A future where Americans will not only tolerate the intrusion, but welcome it.

Quade rolled his eyes when Theodore muttered something while drifting in and out of consciousness about millions of parents murdering their children in utero. Then Theodore's final sentence arrived. He pieced together a disjointed string of slurred words about internment camps and a great culling of American citizens, then fell silent.

Seizing upon the long awaited opportunity, Quade wasted no time standing, picking up his chair, and quietly placing it out of the way before pausing at the door.

Looking over his shoulder he felt a tinge of guilt about how he just treated Theodore. Watching him struggle to breathe—his chest rising and falling violently with every breath he drew—Quade took pity on his friend whose appearance he no longer recognized and whose mind he no longer envied.

Julia was pushing a cart of medications past Theodore's room when Quade finally emerged.

"Oh, hello," she said as she brought the cart to a halt. "I'm sorry about the interruption, but Theo needed his medication."

"Don't worry; you didn't interrupt anything."

"I wanted to thank you for stopping by. He doesn't receive many visitors."

"Sure," Quade said. "I try to pop in now and then whenever I get the chance."

"Over the years I've seen countless people in his condition, but unlike Theo, they all had family and friends by their side."

"He did that to himself," Quade said as he gazed down the hallway toward the exit. "I've never met a man so committed to his work. His entire life revolved around his career. He never made time for a family, or even close friends. Ever since I met him, I aspired to be as good of a journalist as him, but if that means I have to make the sacrifices he did, then maybe I'm not so sure that is a goal worth achieving."

"Losing yourself in work seems to be more common nowadays, and now your friend has few people here for him in his greatest time of need."

"It doesn't look like he's going to make it much longer."

"I'm afraid you're right."

"Well, I'll try to stop by next week."

"He'll appreciate that," Julia said while fiddling with a medicine bottle. "Thanks again for coming by today."

"It was my pleasure," Quade said as he turned to walk away.

"Oh," Julia called out, "if I don't see you next week, have a happy Thanksgiving."

"You too."

SEVEN

Quade had much work to do at the office but his favorite delicatessen in all of Atlanta was near the hospital and he needed to quench the hunger in his belly if he hoped to make it through the rest of the day. The owner of the deli—a jovial, grey-haired man who was considered an artist at making sandwiches—was always good for a new joke each time Quade stopped in. And right now Quade welcomed the distraction from the gnawing thoughts of his own mortality.

After devouring a Reuben on fresh baked rye, laughing at a couple new jokes, and an exchange about the weather, Quade left satiated and ready for the drive back to work.

Quade's fellow journalists were sure to ask how his visit with Theodore went, so during the drive he rehearsed how he was going to break the news to them about their former colleague's dementia without sounding callous.

By nature journalists are drawn to stories—the more sensational the better—but this lurid gossip he was about to spill pertained to someone they all knew . . . someone who was dying.

Quade was whistling as he climbed the stairwell of the office building but when he entered the newsroom the whistling stopped. The air was buzzing with commotion and Quade immediately sensed the tension in the room.

Every reporter was on a phone. Cradling the receivers in the crooks of their necks, some banged away at their typewriters while others feverishly scribbled in their notepads. One man appeared catatonic while holding a hand over his mouth. A woman was crying.

Unable to distinguish what was causing all the distress, Quade stood by his desk feeling isolated among the cacophony of troubled voices.

A young mail clerk who looked as shaken as everyone else was walking past Quade.

"Winston!" Quade said as he grabbed the man's arm, "What's going on?"

The man swallowed hard before answering. "President Kennedy was just shot in Dallas."

Quade's heart pounded in his ears while the rest of his body became paralyzed. When he regained his composure, Winston was gone but the chaos remained.

Feeling sick to his stomach, Quade took a seat at his desk. He couldn't just sit there though, he needed to take action. But what? He should make a phone call. But to whom?

He was still processing the situation and what his next step would be when his boss interrupted the room demanding everyone's attention. "I just got off the phone with my contact in Dallas," he said. "President Kennedy has just been pronounced dead."

"No . . . no . . . no . . . ," Quade whispered to himself before knocking over his chair as he sprung from his desk. He dashed down the stairs to his car and sped out of the parking lot.

Quade double parked outside the hospital and sprinted inside, not slowing until Julia intercepted him outside Theodore's room.

"I need in," he demanded, "I must see Theo."

"I'm sorry," she said, "but you can't do that."

"What?"

"Theodore just passed away a few minutes ago."

Covering his face with both hands, Quade collapsed to the floor, resting his back against the wall. "I am truly sorry for your loss," said Julia, kneeling beside him.

"He could have stopped this."

"There's nothing anyone could have done. You know that. It was his time."

"No!" Quade said sobbing. "President Kennedy."

"Oh, yes. The whole country is in shock right now."

"He could have prevented it."

"Who could have prevented what?"

"Theo knew Kennedy was going to be assassinated."

"Look, I know you're distraught over the loss of your friend but—"

"He knew about it for years but did nothing to stop it."

Julia said nothing more. She stood and looked around. Catching the eye of Dr. O'Brien, she waved him over. She and the doctor helped Quade to his feet, walked him to a nearby room, and placed him on a bed while he repeated the story that he heard from Theodore.

Julia rolled up one of Quade's sleeves while the doctor prepared a syringe.

"And if Theo was right about this," Quade continued, "then all the other things he mentioned will happen too."

"The whole nation is under stress right now," Dr. O'Brien said in a calm tone as he drove the needle into Quade's arm.

"This will help you to relax," Julia added as the doctor pushed the plunger.

"I didn't believe him . . . I didn't believe him," Quade lamented.

Once the needle was removed, Dr. O'Brien leaned in close to Quade's ear. "Everything will be all right," he whispered. "You have nothing to worry about. This is America. Those things will never happen here."

The End.

A note from the author, J.L. Pattison:

Thank you for reading *Saving Kennedy*. If you enjoyed this book I'd be profoundly grateful if you left me a review on Amazon and Goodreads as well as telling your friends about it on social media.

Both of these stories contained in *Saving Kennedy* (*Alibi Interrupted* and *The Visitor*) are also available individually as e-books.

Other stories by J.L. Pattison coming soon:

THE ISLAND
When a clandestine intelligence gathering team sneaks onto a small island under the cover of darkness, the operation goes horribly wrong. Only one man is left to complete the mission, however, the information that he was intending to gather pales in comparison to what he soon discovers is actually happening on the island.

COLLISION
The lives of three vastly different people intersect in the span of a few minutes as each one views the other through a different set of eyes, and proves that people aren't always what they seem.

REVOLUTION FROM A PARK BENCH
A strange man on a city park bench begins to draw the attention of countless people. Because his actions are so strange, no one dares approach the man until one day a young boy breaks from the crowd and takes a seat next to the stranger.

CHASING HER

A desperate man trying to catch a mysterious woman doesn't realize that he too is being pursued.

IN SEARCH OF GREENER GRASS

A man takes his family on a journey into the unknown universe in search of a habitable planet hoping to find an escape from the wars of home. But the grass isn't always greener, even on other planets.

A MAN NAMED ED

A mother answers the door to discover a mysterious man on her doorstep. He offers to take her son, free of charge, into his care to train him, educate him, and prepare him for the future, but is the man's proposition too good to be true?

THE UNREQUITED

In the 1940s, a woman has a chance to meet with her former husband in a train station as he's passing through her town. After years of separation she has dreamed of this opportunity to—not only ask his forgiveness for what she did to destroy their marriage—but to hopefully rekindle their love.

However, much has changed in her life during their years apart, including the accident, the result of which makes her reluctant to meet him. Is it better to meet him and take the chance of being rejected, or not show up at all and let him always remember her how she used to be?

THE ROOM

A man awakens in a windowless room not knowing who he is, where he is, or how he got there. Every morning he finds food left for him but as each day passes the room gets smaller. The only means of escape is a single door that remains locked from the outside.

THE GREAT AMERICAN CLUBHOUSE FIRE
A seemingly innocent rivalry between suburban neighborhood boys turns bad when one group burns down the other group's clubhouse and a body is found inside.

THE DAY BENNY DIED
After years of conversations between two women in the state prison, one of them finally confesses to the other about her part in a murder from decades earlier.

THE MONSTER IN THE WELL
Jack has a secret. He keeps a monster in an old well. As long as it stays in the well it's harmless, but if it escapes it will destroy all of mankind. The monster has remained captive for many years until the day Jack tells a neighbor of his secret.

CHAMBERS
A young boy finds himself in an enclosed chamber with one glass wall that looks into two other chambers, each containing one occupant. Everything seems fine until the wall in the third chamber opens.

THE TOWN
A writer for a travel magazine is given an assignment to visit a town in the middle of the Nevada desert that is rumored to be run by Satan. Once the writer arrives he is shocked at what he discovers.

THE MAN IN THE CHAIR
In a chair in the middle of the room, a man sits quietly as his failures are revealed to him with the most brutal of honesty.

THE FARMER IN SHACKLES
A simple farmer sets out to do some work on his property when he draws the attention of a stranger who gives him some shocking news.

WHILE YOU WERE GONE
A woman discovers her entire family missing and a stranger in her kitchen.

THE DREAMS OF EVIL MEN
An old man's been plagued with vividly realistic nightmares. In every dream he is partaking in the genocide of innocents from throughout the annals of history. Is his condition just a matter of psychosis or something far more sinister?

THE TIME ASSASSIN
When the inventors of a time machine are propositioned by the biggest investor in their project to go back in time to commit an assassination, the mission becomes more complicated than they expected.

THE LITTLE GIRL AT THE DOOR
A little girl wishes to bring a gift of life to her dying aunt but is delayed by her parents. Will the little girl be too late when she finally arrives?

FEEDING DRAGONS
Everyone in Poe's village receives a baby dragon when they're born that stays with them for life. But when Poe wants to slay his dragon the villagers cannot understand why.

THE RED BRIDGE
While in search of Eternal City, a kingdom whose inhabitants live forever, two travelers discover that the city lies on the other side of a great chasm and is accessed by only two bridges. However, neither man can agree on which of the bridges to take and neither man is willing to yield to the other because picking the wrong bridge will prove deadly.